A Sort-of Sailor

Amy Hest

Illustrated by

Lizzy Rockwell

Four Winds Press
New York

Four Winds Press
Macmillan Publishing Company
866 Third Avenue, New York, NY 10022
Collier Macmillan Canada, Inc.
Printed and bound in Hong Kong
First American Edition

10   9   8   7   6   5   4   3   2   1

The text of this book is set in 14 point Weidemann Book.
The illustrations are rendered in watercolor.

Library of Congress Cataloging-in-Publication Data
Hest, Amy. A sort-of sailor/Amy Hest;
illustrated by Lizzy Rockwell. — 1st American ed.   p.   cm.
Summary: Nell and her brother, Theo, love their family's
new boat from the start, but their mother must
make a heroic effort to conquer her fear of boating.
ISBN 0-02-743641-1
[1. Boats and boating — Fiction. 2. Fear — Fiction.]
I. Rockwell, Lizzy, ill. II. Title.
PZ7.H4375So   1990   [E] — dc20
89-38252   CIP   AC

H469s

For my father, who was
a special sort of sailor
— A.H.

For John
— L.R.

The boat was my father's idea.
He had all the ideas that had something to do with fun.

"Bought us a present," he announced one day.

"A dog!" I guessed.

"You've already got one, Nell."

"A car!" My brother, Theo, who was twelve, had only one thing on his brain in those days.

"I suppose it's going to be something sensible?" said my mother. Now, my mother knew it wasn't going to be sensible. She knew it would be something to do with fun.

Probably she was thinking about the time my father did something that was really fun (in my opinion, not hers). That was the time he brought home five new puppies, all in a barrel. Those puppies were cuter than bunnies! We only got to keep one, though. Pizza-Man. The rest went straight to the relatives in Brooklyn. My mother, who was not a big dog lover, yet, said—and she said it loud and clear—"One dog is enough for me!"

"Everyone in sneakers," called my father. "Right away, quick!"

"How about tomorrow?" teased my mother.

"Aren't you even curious?" my father teased back.

"Well, maybe just a little."

So, all sneakered and curious, we piled into the car and we drove. Only my father knew anything about where we were going or why we were going there.

We drove on the highway.

We drove through a sleepy little village that smelled like fish.

We drove past a blinking yellow light.

We bumped across a rocky driveway, and then we piled out.

"Hmmm, what is this?" My mother was looking suspicious and she was looking all around.

"Hmmm, what do you think?" My father answered her question with his, and with a smile that was a little like a kid's.

"What I think is, this looks like a boatyard and there are plenty of *boats*." My mother's lips got all twisty the way they do when she is getting ready to cry or yell.

My father led the way.

I skipped at his heels, across a maze of wooden docks. My mother was right—boats were everywhere! They were big and small, tall and tiny. Spanking white, and needing paint. The whole world seemed to shimmer in the late-May light.

"Ta-da-a!" My father stopped beside a boat that looked... well... *tired* in the water. It was biggish. Oldish. Run-down, too.

"Ta-da-a?" That was my mother.

My father was all proud and gloating, though, and his hazel eyes were dancing. "You'll love it," he said, holding her hand.

"Don't think so, Cye."

"Try," he coaxed, and he kissed the tip of her nose.

"Come on aboard!" Theo waved his arms. That boy was awfully happy for someone whose specialty was cars.

"You know," my mother whispered, "I've never been on a boat before. Except maybe a canoe."

I stepped aside to eye this boat that was our boat. I liked it already! I liked the way it bobbed in the water and the little round portholes covered over with checkered curtains. I wondered who put them there. Cozy, I thought, curtains on a boat.

It was moored to the pier with fraying ropes. They stretched and slackened, stretched and slackened, making strange creaking sounds. There were those sounds and others. Like the gentle lapping of water. And overhead a seagull shrieked, then made wide, dipping figure eights in the sky. Show-off!

My father gave us the grand tour.

"Sleeps four," he boasted.

"Sleep on a boat?" my mother croaked.

"Is this a *kitchen*?" asked Theo.

"Galley," said my father. "On a ship it's called a galley."

"Tiny," sniffed my mother.

"Efficient!" My father opened and closed seven skinny cabinets. Each one had a curvy brass handle.

"A baby bathroom!" I hooted from way up front.

"Head," I was told. "On a ship it's called a head."

Immediately after the grand tour, my father handed me a wide, flat paintbrush. He passed a quart of paint that said BOAT PAINT to Theo and brass polish to my mother. Lifting a hatch, he pointed to a big, old, crusty-looking engine. "Needs love." He sighed. "Needs work, too."

"Now, what do you know about engines?" My
mother's arms were folded and her foot was tapping away.
Tap tap. Tap tap tap.

"What I know is, I need to know more." My father
whipped out a handbook. "I'm all signed up for school,"
he said. "I intend to be the best sea captain around. No
matter who else is around."

What we didn't know then was my father's other intention. To get us *all* in shape. Shipshape. He insisted on sharing this new language of his. The language of boats. He talked. He explained. He reexplained. He even gave pop quizzes, and it was usually over dessert.

"Theo, where is the *bow* of the ship?"

"Front!"

"Nell, the back is called ...?"

"Stern, Daddy!"

Once or twice he opened his mouth to ask my mother a boat question. But she gave him a look, and he changed his mind fast.

The boat. Weeks later—painted, polished, and mechanically sound—we christened her the *Mal de Mer*. That's a French name and it means "seasick." My mother thought it up.

We had a little party. Theo and I gave my father a present. A captain's cap. My mother stitched his name across.

On a perfect Sunday in August, we cruised past rows of docks. Through narrow channels. Into a wide channel that felt like the ocean. It wasn't, though. It was just a bay.

Finally. The maiden voyage of the *Mal de Mer*!

My father, the captain, at the helm.

My mother, hunched over a huge chart that flapped and billowed in the wind. (She battened it down with her elbows.)

Theo, fooling with the ship-to-shore radio. "This is the *Mal de Mer*, the *Mal de Mer*, heading due east, seven knots…"

Soon the sun was high and hot. Seagulls rose and swooped and dunked for fish and cried their seagull cries.

"Follow!" I sang. "Follow! Follow!"

Some of them did.

Later I shimmied along the catwalk, hoisting myself up
top. I sat there a long, long time, watching the blue-green
water all around and the boats and clouds.

"Are you all right?" called my mother. Her hair was
coming unclipped and it was wild. Pretty, though.

"Come on up, Mama!"

"Me? Up there?" Her eyes got big and wide. "Not on
your life!"

Her words whooshed past my ears and the wind filled them and pushed long strands of copper in my face. And I laughed because ... well ... just because.

"Come on up!" I said it again, laughing.

This time she did. Super-slow. Chewing her lip. Not looking down. Not looking up. Step by sneakered step.

And there we sat, nice and close, knees up, leaning back against the dinghy in the sun.

"I love it!" I cried. "Don't you?"

"Not exactly, Nell."

"I wish you would."

"I'm trying," she said, and there was something in the way she said it that made me think she was trying more than a little, and probably a whole lot.

"You've never been on a boat before the *Mal de Mer*," I remembered. "Except maybe a canoe."

She frowned.

"Well, maybe it just takes getting used to," I said.

"Maybe."

"Mama?"

"Mm-hmm?"

"Are you *afraid*?"

"I guess maybe a little."

A grown-up afraid? What next? I thought.

"It makes no sense at all," sighed my mother, "but sometimes a person is just plain scared."

I thought about that.

"Like me in the dark when I was little. Remember?" I said. "That made no sense either, but there I was, scared in the dark!"

"You do understand." My mother made a circle on my knee with her finger. Then a heart.

Suddenly the *Mal de Mer* pitched and dipped and I
held on to my mother and she held on to me, and I was
wishing for a shore—any shore—and I bet she was, too.

"Ahoy, mates!" hollered my father from the helm.
"Everything okay up there?"

"What do you think," I hollered back, "we're a couple
of landlubbers or something?"

We dropped anchor in a quiet cove tucked out of the
way of fishing boats and speeding boats and fancy
yachting boats. All around were families like our family
and kids squealing and swimming and rowing their
dinghies and rafts.

"Lunch, mates!" My mother brought up sandwiches
from the galley. Chicken and egg salad and my favorite,
salami. The red-striped thermos was filled with her special
brand of iced tea. It had plenty of sugar and a slight
lemon tang.

In the afternoon we went swimming. I was fearless! I
jumped in. I dove in. I cannonballed, too. Afterward they
wrapped me in a towel with anchors on the borders. I
shook until the sun warmed me through and the goose
bumps disappeared. I licked at the backs of my hands,
saltier than the sea.

My father took Theo rowing in the dinghy.

Then he took me.

"Mama's afraid," I said. "She's no great sailor either."

"But she is a good sport," said my father. "World-class."

"Tries hard, too. Who knows"—I giggled—"she might wind up a sort-of sailor. Someday."

"You better believe it! She's got a gutsy streak, your mother. Braver than you think." My father wrinkled his nose and he smiled. "I love that about her."

"Me, too," I said.

Way later, we cruised home as the sun sank slowly toward the water. Slivers of pink and yellow crisscrossed the low summer sky. We slipped into sweatshirts: the bright sunshine had made our skin burn and chill at the same time. And the breeze off the choppy bay blew cold air in our faces.

My father, the captain, backed into the dock. By now
the sky was pitch black, stars were glittery and winking. I
fell asleep on my mother's lap.

She was humming.